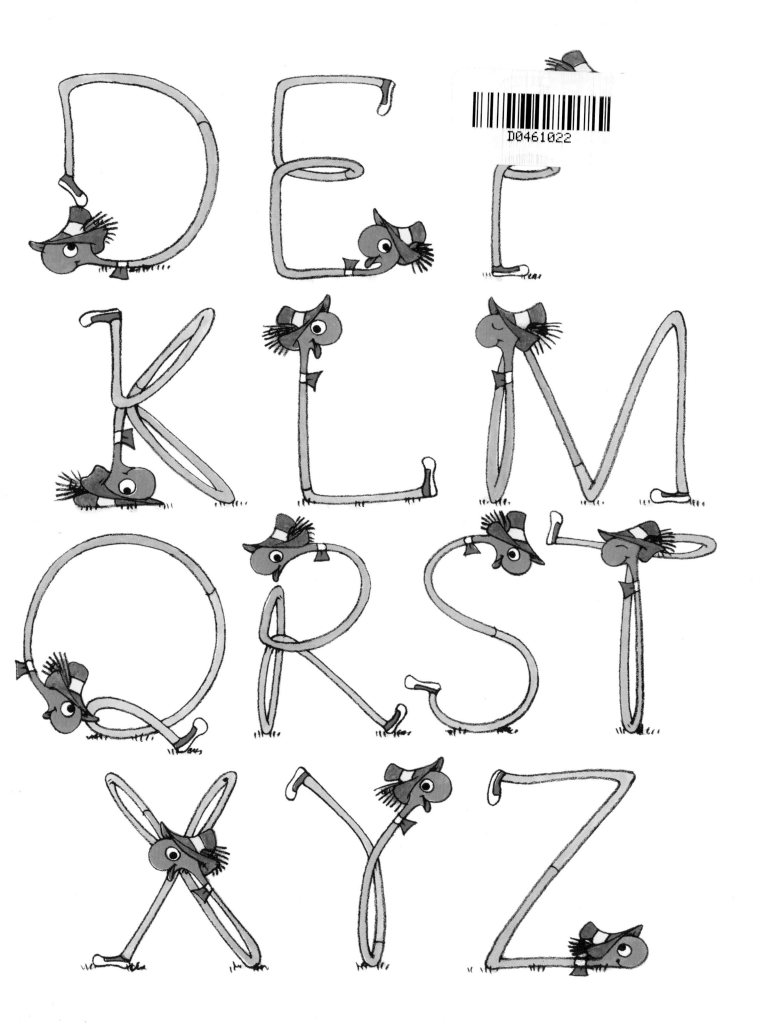

This book belongs to

....

....

A GOLDEN BOOK • NEW YORK
Copyright © 2013 by the Richard Scarry Corporation.
All rights reserved.
This 2014 edition was published in the United States by Golden Books, an imprint of Random House
Children's Books, a division of Random House LLC, 1745 Broadway, New York, NY 10019, and in
Canada by Random House of Canada Limited, Toronto, Penguin Random House Companies.
Originally published in Great Britain by HarperCollins UK, London, in 2013.

Golden Books and the G colophon are registered trademarks of Random House LLC.

Visit us on the Web!
randomhouse.com/kids/richardscarry

Educators and librarians, for a variety of teaching tools, visit us at RHTeachersLibrarians.com

Library of Congress Cataloging-in-Publication Data is available upon request.
ISBN 978-0-385-38782-8 (trade) — ISBN 978-0-385-38783-5 (ebook)

MANUFACTURED IN CHINA

First American Edition

10 9 8 7 6 5 4 3 2 1

Random House Children's Books supports the First Amendment and celebrates the right to read.

Richard Scarry's

BEST LOWLY WORM BOOK

EVER!

A GOLDEN BOOK • NEW YORK

LOWLY

BOOK

Richard Scarry's
BEST
WORM
EVER!

Good Morning, Lowly!

I am a worm. My name is Lowly Worm.

I get up in the morning
and wash my face and foot.

It's a little bit difficult,
but I can dress myself.

Everyone helps make breakfast at the Cat family house, where I live.

After breakfast, Huckle, Sally, and I clear the table.

Daddy Cat washes the dishes.

We make our beds.

Hey!
Where is Lowly?

We tidy our rooms and hang up our clothes.

Then we say goodbye to Mommy Cat and go to the school bus stop.

Off to School

We are careful crossing the road.
We look both ways.

We walk and do not run.

We say "Good morning" to
the school bus driver.

We sit quietly in our
seats on the way to
school. Arthur shows me
his new toy police car.

I bring an apple to
Miss Honey, the schoolteacher.

Huckle draws a
picture of me.

I help Sally
string beads.

I show and tell a story
to my classmates.

I empty the wastebasket.

My, it is windy!

The school doctor examines my throat. Ahhhh!

I write on the board.

I am a school crossing guard, and I help the children cross the road safely!

This Is Me

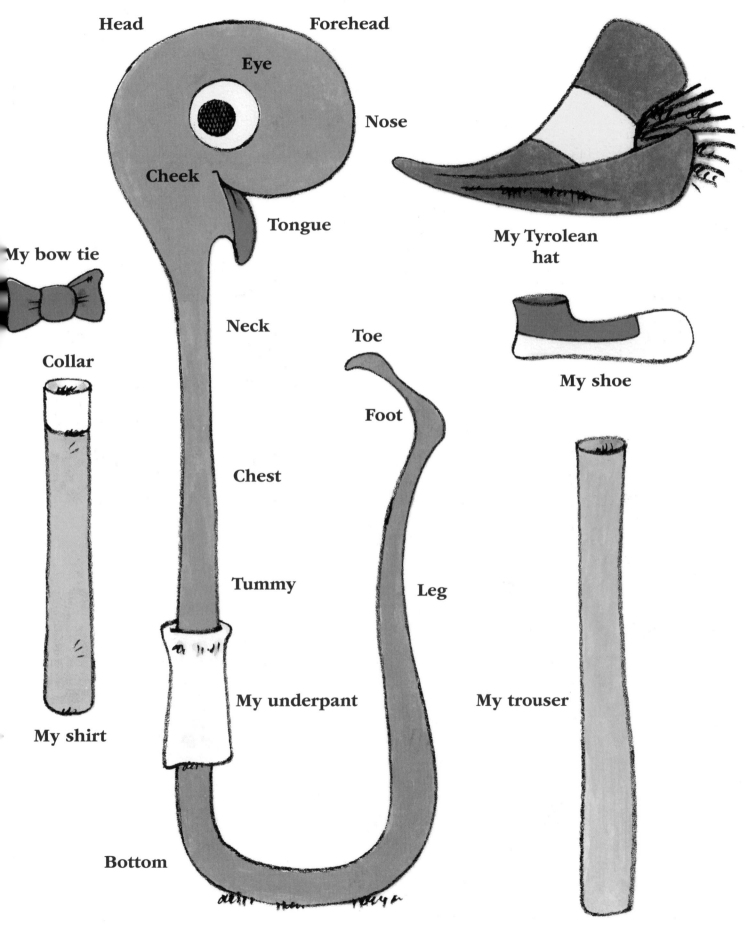

Head

Forehead

Eye

Nose

Cheek

Tongue

My Tyrolean
hat

My bow tie

Neck

Toe

My shoe

Collar

Foot

Chest

Tummy

Leg

My underpant

My trouser

Bottom

My shirt

Lowly's Good Manners

Everyone should have
good manners.

When I want something,
I say "Please."

When something is given
to me, I say "Thank you."

I hold the door open for others.

I don't interrupt when
others are talking.

I help do
the dishes.

I am a good
helper. I help tie
shoelaces.

I sit up straight at the table.
Sometimes I forget to take off my hat.

I always wait
my turn.

I don't push or shove others.

I share my things.

I never fight, for that is very bad manners.

I read stories to
younger children.

When I leave after a visit to someone's house,
I always say "Thank you for a very nice time."

Counting with Lowly

I can count! You can, too!

1 One Lowly Worm driving

2 Two cats smiling

3 Three pigs crying

4 Four dogs barking

5 Five foxes sleeping

6 Six mice honking

honk!

honk! honk! honk! honk! honk!

7 Seven frogs swimming

8 Eight rabbits running

9 Nine crows singing

10 Ten bugs jumping

11
Eleven horn blowers playing

12
Twelve skiers skiing

13
Thirteen hikers hiking

14
Fourteen sledders sledding

15
Fifteen cars driving

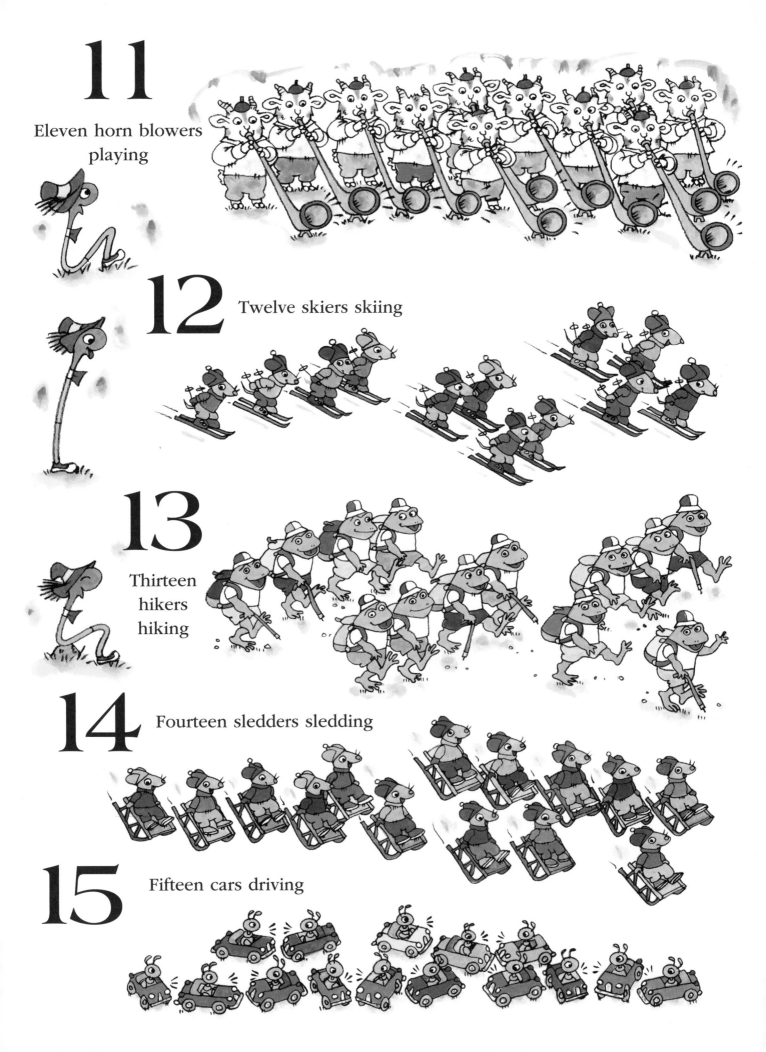

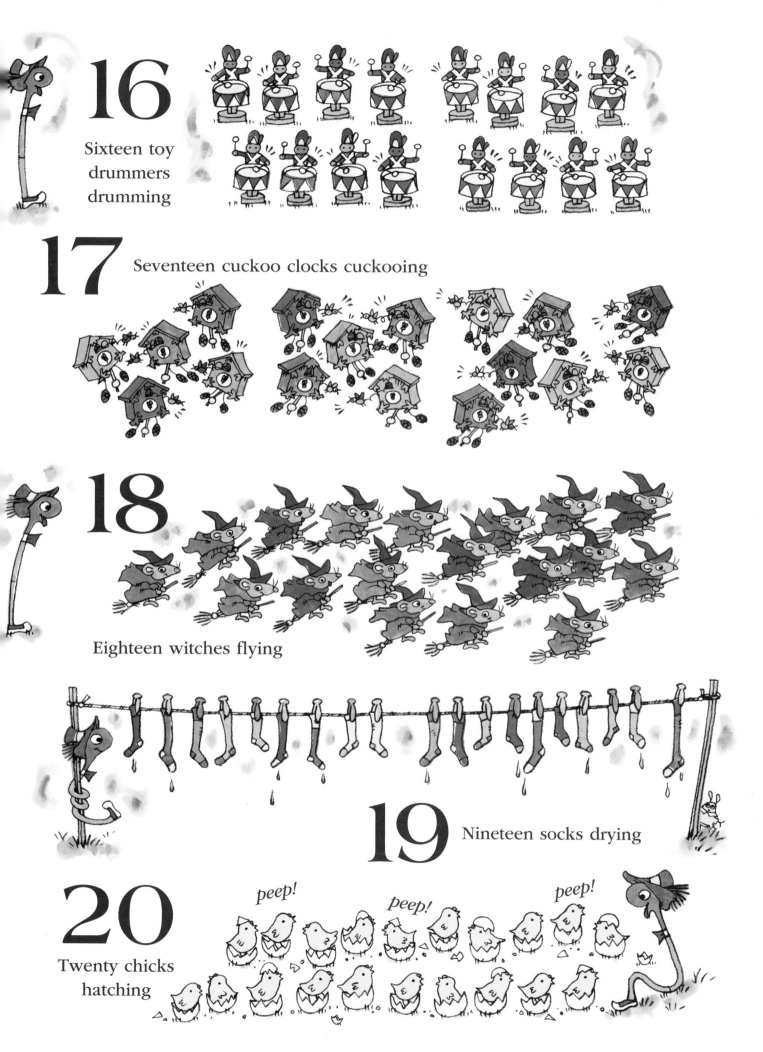

16

Sixteen toy
drummers
drumming

17

Seventeen cuckoo clocks cuckooing

18

Eighteen witches flying

19

Nineteen socks drying

20

Twenty chicks
hatching

peep! *peep!* *peep!*

A Visit to Farmer Pig

It is fun to visit Farmer Pig's farm.

We plow the field.

We plant the seeds.

I water the plants.

I gather the eggs from the henhouse. Sometimes I drop an egg or two. Oops! Sorry, Farmer Pig!

I pump water for Mrs. Pig.

I pick apples from the apple tree.

I help Farmer Pig bring his apples to the market.

Meanwhile, the corn has grown tall! When the corn is ripe, we all sit down to eat a delicious picnic.

Hop Aboard with Lowly!

I like to take trips.

Sometimes I fly in my apple copter.

Sometimes I fly a light plane.

Other times, I fly a big jet plane.

SWISSAIR

A motorboat can go very fast over the water.

I am always happy sailing my little sailboat.

A submarine can go on top of the water or under the water.

To visit outer space, I travel in a space capsule.

GSTAAD MY LOVE

Sometimes I fly in my apple balloon! It's fun!

Trains speed along the tracks from town to town and from city to city.

To get around the neighborhood, I ride my bike!

My apple car takes me on many trips in the country.

Busy Workers on the Go

I am a busy worker.
I help other busy
workers do their jobs.

I help Milly the milk lady
deliver her bottles of milk.

Smokey and Squirty
let me ride on the
fire engine!

I cruise about with
Officer Simpson in the police car.

Cleaner Casey and I
clean the streets.

I help Postman Pig deliver the mail.

Big Gussie and I pick up the rubbish around town.

Rikki and I drive the children to school.

Taxis drive here, there, and everywhere.

I deliver eggs for Farmer Pig. Sometimes I break one or two. Oops! Sorry, Farmer Pig!

Things I Can Do.
Can You Do Them, Too?

These are some of the things I can do:

I can crawl.

I can hop.

I can kneel.

I can sit.

I can ride.

I can read.

I can draw.

I can also stand
on my head.

I can run.

I can eat.

I can kick.

I can laugh.

I can swim.

I can talk.

Where's Lowly?

I like to play hide-and-seek.
Can you find me?

Am I in the attic?

In the bedroom?

In the wardrobe?

In the kitchen?

Am I in the bathroom?

On the patio?

In the basement?

At the playground?

Am I in the hall?

In the garage?

In the garden?

On the clothesline?

Am I in the field?

In the apple tree?

In the frog pond?

In the workshop?

Where am I?

Good Night, Lowly!

A busy day is almost done!

Some evenings, Daddy Cat plays
ball with us in the yard.

Then sometimes we
watch television.

We help set the supper table.

And we tell each other
what we did that day.

Then it's time for a bath!

I brush my teeth.

Afterward, Daddy Cat
reads us a story.

Then it's time for bed.

Good night, everyone!
Sleep tight!

See you in
the morning!

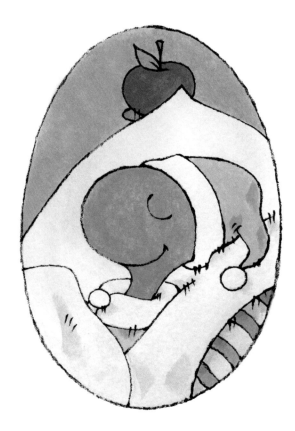